Do You Know How Much I Love You?

by Donna Tedesco

Bradbury Press • New York

Maxwell Macmillan Canada Toronto
Maxwell Macmillan International
New York Oxford Singapore Sydney

Bradbury Press
Macmillan Publishing Company
866 Third Avenue
New York, NY 10022

Maxwell Macmillan Canada, Inc.
1200 Eglinton Avenue East
Suite 200
Don Mills, Ontario M3C 3N1

Macmillan Publishing Company is part of the Maxwell Communication
Group of Companies.
First edition
Printed and bound in the United States of America
Printed on recycled paper
10 9 8 7 6 5 4 3 2 1
The text of this book is set in ITC Caslon 224 Book.
The illustrations are rendered in watercolor.

LIBRARY OF CONGRESS CATALOGING-IN-PUBLICATION DATA

Tedesco, Donna.
Do you know how much I love you? / by Donna Tedesco.—1st ed.
p. cm.
Summary: The unending love of a parent for a child is described in terms that continue to grow.
ISBN 0-02-789120-8
[1. Love—Fiction. 2. Parent and child—Fiction.] I. Title.
PZ7.T226Do 1994
[E]—dc20 92-7856

For Bill and James

—D.T.

I love you more than . . .

all of the petals…

on all of the flowers . . .

in all of the gardens…

in all of the yards…

on all of the blocks...

in all of the neighborhoods...

in all of the towns...

and all of the cities...

in all of the countries…

in the whole wide world.